To Stacey.
Thanks for spreadin
the sweetness!

COOKIE PAWS

Written by **Edwin W. Jorden**

Illustrated by **Valerie J. Waywell**

Gilded Dog Enterprises, LLC

Published by:
Gilded Dog Enterprises LLC
106 High Point Drive
Churchville, PA 18966

Visit us on the web!
www.cookiepaws.com

This children's series is dedicated to our four-legged friends,
who teach us more by their actions
than we could ever learn through speech.

A portion of the proceeds from the sale of this book will be donated to the Humane Society.

Cookie Paws

Who are they?

What are they?

What do they do?

Are they treats you can eat...

...and shaped really neat?

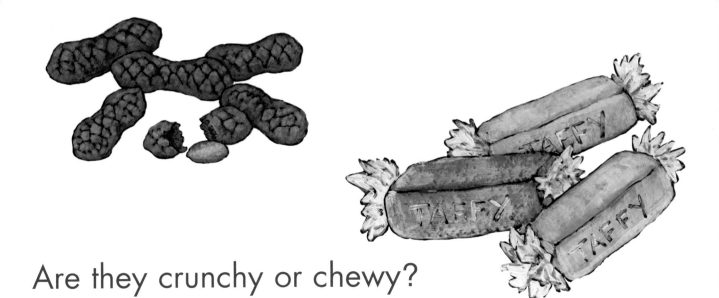

Are they crunchy or chewy?

Are they salty or sweet?

Can you dunk them in milk

or hot cocoa with cream?

Can you eat them by one...

...two

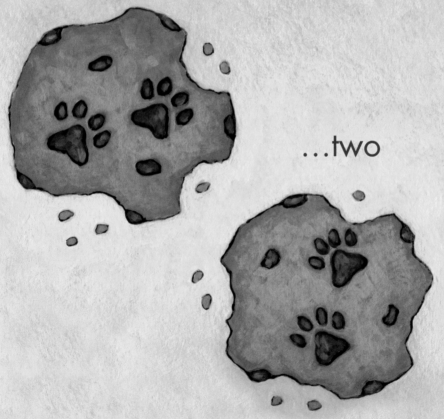

and then three?

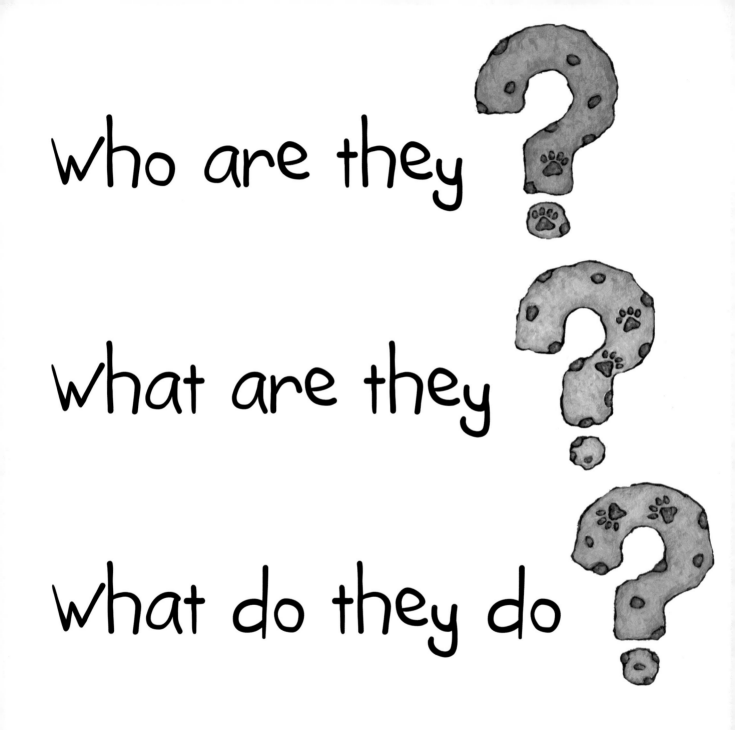

who are they ?

what are they ?

what do they do ?

Could you please tell me?
I haven't a clue!

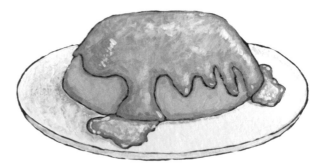

Well,

while their names sound like sweets,

'Sweet Potater Pie' and 'Crème Caramel,'

their sweetness lies mainly inside themselves.

For Sweet Potater Pie and Crème Caramel, Tater and Carrie we'll call them for short, are two doggies whose paws smell like cookies of course.

But why, you may ask,
        do their paws smell so sweet?

What makes them smell
    like the cookies we eat?

As the story goes,
their sweetness inside them
flowed so throughout,
that some of that sweetness
finally seeped out…

...and onto their paws
that sweetness did seep,

so wherever they walked
a trail of sweetness they'd leave.

So, if you see Tater and Carrie
on their adventures to come,

you may find yourself
go from a walk to a run.

About the author

Edwin Jorden graduated from University of Rhode Island, with a Bachelor of Arts in English. For most of his life, he has reveled in the art of creative writing, both as a means of expression and a tool for education. His writing consists primarily of poetry and short-story prose. With his work in children's stories, he hopes to show the value in being kind to all forms of life and supporting those in need.

About the illustrator

After graduating from the Fashion Institute of Technology, Valerie Waywell attended Rowan University followed by the Pennsylvania Academy of Fine Art, where she decided to make painting a full-time career. Through the eyes of an artist, she enjoys the constant change and exploration that life affords. As a result, her work is a product of her surroundings mixed with the hues and tones of her imagination. In addition to illustrations, Valerie has produced a myriad of paintings, from murals and decorative finishes, to oils, acrylics, and pastels which have been featured in various galleries.
She currently resides with her family in Cape May County, New Jersey.

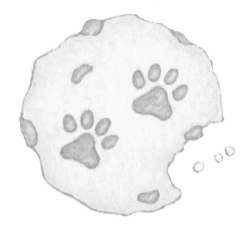